Me Baby!

by Riki Levinson
pictures by Marylin Hafner

Dutton Children's Books   New York

Library of Congress Cataloging-in-Publication Data

Levinson, Riki.
Me baby! / by Riki Levinson; pictures by Marylin Hafner.—1st ed.
p.   cm.
Summary: Danny seeks attention when his aunts and uncles
come over to see his new baby sister.
ISBN 0-525-44693-1
[1. Babies—Fiction.   2. Brothers and sisters—Fiction.]
I. Hafner, Marylin, ill.   II. Title.
PZ7.L5796Me   1991
[E]—dc20   90-40372   CIP   AC

Published in the United States by
Dutton Children's Books,
a division of Penguin Books USA Inc.

Editor: Ann Durell

Printed in Hong Kong by South China Printing Co.
First Edition   10 9 8 7 6 5 4 3 2 1

to family

R.L.

for my daughter Jennifer

M.H.

Danny watched through the window. Aunt Sarah and Uncle Ben and Aunt Cora and Uncle Len were coming!

He ran to the door to meet them.
Danny put his arms up high.

"What a big boy you are!" Aunt Sarah said loudly.
She gave him a kiss and went into the kitchen.

"*Me* baby," Danny said,
dropping his arms.

"What did he say?" asked Aunt Cora. "I can never understand him."

"See baby," Uncle Ben answered. He patted Danny on the head.

"Me *baby*," said Danny.

He put his arms up high again.

"Hi there, Buster," said Uncle Len. He tickled Danny
as he passed him.

Nobody picked up Danny.

Uncle Ben shook hands with Danny's father. Uncle
Len clapped him on the shoulder. Aunt Sarah hugged
and kissed him.

"Where is she?" Aunt Cora asked.

"She'll be up in a minute," answered Danny's father.

"*Me baby!*" yelled Danny.

"Shhhh, Danny," his father warned.

"Me baby," whispered Danny.

He climbed up on the couch.
Danny put his thumb in his mouth.
He pulled his soft blanket against his cheek
and rocked.

"*Here* she is," sang Danny's mother, bringing the baby in.

Everyone crowded around them. Everyone except Danny.

"Me baby," Danny said, unhappily.
Nobody heard him.

"Did you ever?" said Aunt Sarah as she took
the baby. "Why, she looks just like you, Sam."

Danny slid off the couch.
He ran to Aunt Sarah and
pulled at her skirt.

"Mmmm, mmmm, mmmm," cooed Aunt Cora,
taking the baby from Aunt Sarah.

Danny reached up and pulled Aunt Cora's arm.
"Does he want the baby? You're too little,"
Aunt Cora said.
"Me baby," said Danny.

"Kitchy, kitchy, koo," said Uncle Ben, taking
the baby from Aunt Cora.

Danny wrapped his arms around his uncle's leg
and pulled.

Uncle Ben didn't even pat him on the head.

"Cute as a button," said Uncle Len, reaching for the baby.

Danny's mother and father hugged.

"ME BABY! ME BABY!"
Danny screamed.

"Waaaa! Waaaa! Waaaa!" cried the baby.
Mother grabbed her.

Danny threw himself on the floor.
"Meeee! Meeee! Meeee!" he cried.

His father heard him.

"You're my Danny," he said,
swooping him up.

They plunked down on the couch.
"My Danny, my Danny," his father said
as he bounced him on his knees.
Danny giggled.

"Anna? Now?" asked his father.

"Yes, Sam," his mother answered softly.

She put the baby on Danny's lap.
Everybody was watching.

"Baby!" Danny screamed, happily. "ME!"